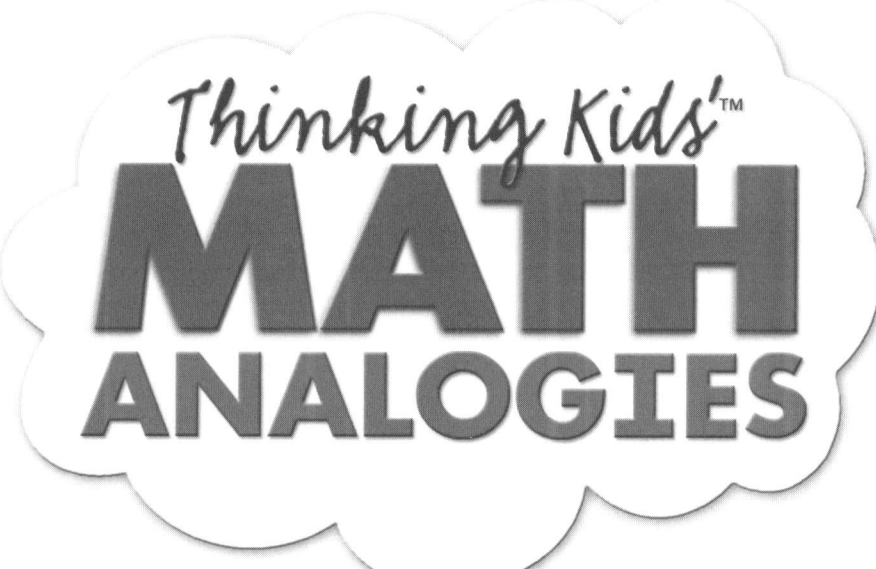

Grade 3

by Leigh Morrison Cox

Carson-Dellosa Publishing LLC
Greensboro, North Carolina

Credits

Content Editor: Amy Gamble

Copy Editor: Karen Seberg

Layout and Cover Design: Lori Jackson

 This book has been correlated to state, common core state, national, and Canadian provincial standards. Visit *www.carsondellosa.com* to search for and view its correlations to your standards.

Carson-Dellosa Publishing LLC
PO Box 35665
Greensboro, NC 27425 USA

ISBN 978-1-936024-19-3

335101151

Table of Contents

Skills Matrix

	Number Sense	Add and Subtract	Multiply and Divide	Place Value	Money	Fractions	Number Relationships	Patterns	Variables and Functions	Length, Weight, and Capacity	Temperature and Time	Perimeter, Area, and Volume	Plane and Solid Figures	Symmetry, Congruence, and Transformations	Coordinate Graphing	Lines, Rays, and Angles	Data Analysis	Probability and Permutations
6	★			★			★											
7	★	★	★	★		★												
8	★	★		★	★	★												
9	★	★	★	★	★													
10	★	★	★			★	★											
11	★	★	★			★												
12	★	★	★				★											
13		★	★		★		★											
14		★	★		★	★												
15		★	★	★	★	★	★											
16	★	★	★		★	★												
17	★	★	★	★		★		★										
18		★	★	★	★	★	★											
19		★					★	★	★									
20			★				★	★	★									
21			★					★	★									
22		★					★	★	★									
23		★	★		★		★	★	★									
24		★	★					★	★									
25		★	★		★			★	★									
26		★	★				★	★	★									
27		★	★					★	★									
28			★					★	★									
29		★	★					★	★									
30													★	★		★		
31													★			★		
32													★	★		★		
33													★	★		★		
34													★			★		
35													★	★	★			
36													★	★				
37													★					
38													★	★		★		
39													★		★	★		
40													★	★	★	★		
41										★	★							
42										★	★							
43										★	★							
44						★				★	★							
45										★	★	★						
46						★				★	★	★						
47						★				★	★	★						
48						★				★	★	★						
49						★				★	★	★						
50						★	★			★	★							
51					★	★				★	★	★						
52																	★	★
53						★											★	★
54																	★	★
55						★												★
56						★											★	★
57																	★	★
58																	★	★
59																	★	★
60																	★	★

Introduction

Problem solving is a critical skill for understanding and applying math concepts. *Thinking Kids'™ Math Analogies* provides students with ample problem-solving practice for thinking analogically while reinforcing standards-based math skills. Analogies build conceptual bridges between what is familiar and what is new.

Thinking Kids'™ Math Analogies contains five sections, one for each content strand of the National Council of Teachers of Mathematics (NCTM) standards: Number and Operations, Algebra, Geometry, Measurement, and Data Analysis and Probability. These sections are ordered by difficulty to build skills and allow for differentiation. The level is indicated by a code at the bottom of each page.

★ Basic: equivalency-based analogies and beginning skills

★ ★ Intermediate: part equivalency-based and part logic-based analogies with more difficult skills

★ ★ ★ Advanced: logic-based analogies with challenging skills

Before students work with the analogies in this book, they will need to be familiar with the format of an analogy and the proper way to read and interpret analogies. You may wish to give students practice with a few simple verbal analogies, such as "*up* is to *down* as *on* is to *off*," before modeling math analogies. Teach students to read an analogy as this:

$$A \underset{\text{is to}}{\colon} B \underset{\text{as}}{\colon\colon} C \underset{\text{is to}}{\colon} D$$

Determine the connection or relationship between A and B on the left side of the double colon (∷). Apply that same connection to find the missing item (D) on the right and to complete the analogy.

Solving mathematical analogies can help students understand mathematical relationships and vocabulary. The *How do you know?* component asks students to write how they solved the analogy. Students should be encouraged to use mathematical vocabulary to explain their thinking.

As students progress through the book, they will not only gain an understanding of analogies but also build a solid mathematics foundation for their future.

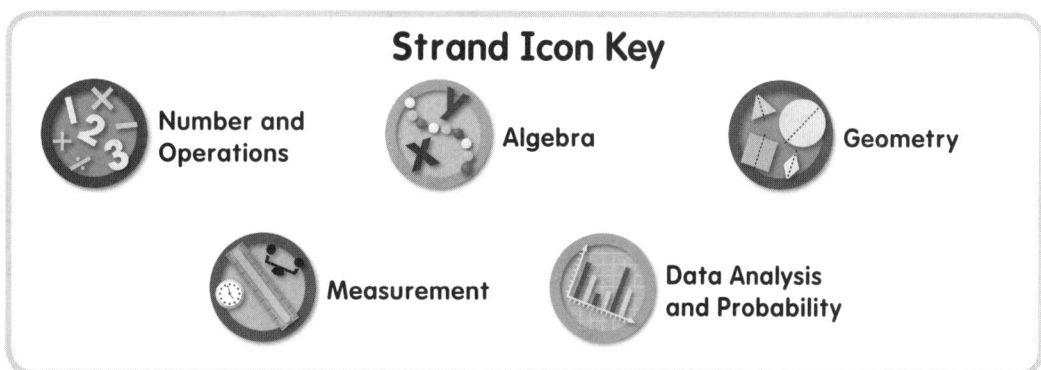

Strand Icon Key

Number and Operations

Algebra

Geometry

Measurement

Data Analysis and Probability

Name _____

Date _____

Complete each analogy and explain your answer.

1 542 : five hundreds :: 783 : _____

How do you know? _____

2 4,825 : 5,000 :: 2,142 : _____

How do you know? _____

3 2,345 2,354 2,453 : least to greatest :: 4,532 4,523 4,352 : _____

How do you know? _____

4 6 hundreds, 15 tens, 4 ones : 754 :: 7 hundreds, 12 tens, 5 ones : _____

How do you know? _____

5 672 : six hundred seventy-two :: 843 : _____

How do you know? _____

Name _____   Date _____

Complete each analogy and explain your answer.

1 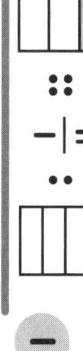 ∷ _____

How do you know? _____

2 4,562 : 4 thousands ∷ 8,275 : _____

How do you know? _____

3 two thousand six hundred forty-one : 2,641 ∷ three thousand five hundred twenty-two : _____

How do you know? _____

4 87,241 : 90,000 ∷ 49,523 : _____

How do you know? _____

5 6 + 6 + 6 + 6 : 6 × 4 ∷ 3 + 3 + 3 + 3 + 3 : _____

How do you know? _____

Name _____

Date _____

Complete each analogy and explain your answer.

1. 6,593 : 6,000 + 500 + 90 + 3 :: 7,924 : _____

_____

How do you know? _____

2.  $\frac{1}{5}$: :: $\frac{1}{8}$:

_____

How do you know? _____

3. 8,791 : 8,800 :: 6,581 : _____

_____

How do you know? _____

4. 3 quarters, 8 dimes, 10 nickels : $2.05 :: 2 quarters, 6 dimes, 8 nickels : _____

_____

How do you know? _____

5. 3 hundreds : 30 tens :: 8 hundreds : _____

_____

How do you know? _____

Number and Operations

8

Name _____

Complete each analogy and explain your answer.

1 8,000 + 700 + 4 : 8,704 :: 6,000 + 50 + 1 : _____

_____

How do you know? _____

2 8 hundreds, 17 tens, 3 ones : 973 :: 9 hundreds, 13 tens, 9 ones : _____

_____

How do you know? _____

3 63 + 11 : 60 + 10 :: 12 + 22 : _____

_____

How do you know? _____

4 8 × 5 : 8 + 8 + 8 + 8 + 8 :: 9 × 3 : _____

_____

How do you know? _____

5 2 quarters, 12 dimes, 5 nickels : $1.95 :: 4 quarters, 15 dimes, 6 nickels : _____

_____

How do you know? _____

Number and Operations

9

★ • © Carson-Dellosa

Name _____

Date _____

Complete each analogy and explain your answer.

1  : greatest to least :: 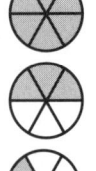 :

_____

How do you know?

_____

2 52 + 21 : 70 :: 41 + 53 :

_____

How do you know?

_____

3  :: $\frac{2}{6}$:

_____

How do you know?

_____

4 XVI : 16 :: XIV :

_____

How do you know?

_____

5 24 ÷ 8 : 8 × 3 :: 30 ÷ 6 :

_____

How do you know?

_____

Number and Operations

10

Name _____   Date _____

Complete each analogy and explain your answer.

1 300 x 7 : 2,100 :: 2,000 x 9 : _____

   How do you know? _____

2 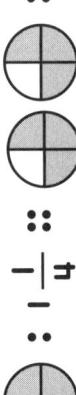 : 1 :: $\frac{1}{4}$ ::

   How do you know? _____

3 3 dozen : 36 :: 5 dozen : _____

   How do you know? _____

4 XXVI – XIX : VII :: XVIII – XIV : _____

   How do you know? _____

5 3 x 2 + 5 : 11 :: 4 x 3 + 7 : _____

   How do you know? _____

Number and Operations   11

Name _____

Complete each analogy and explain your answer.

1   8 × 8 : 64 ÷ 8 :: 6 × 6 : _____

How do you know? _____

2   1,101   1,010   1,001 : greatest to least :: 2,252   2,525   2,552 : _____

How do you know? _____

3   8,756 + 775 : 9,600 :: 4,888 + 263 : _____

How do you know? _____

4   72 ☐ 9 = 8 : divide :: 8 ☐ 7 = 56 : _____

How do you know? _____

5   30 × 60 : 1,800 :: 50 × 90 : _____

How do you know? _____

12

Name _____ Date _____

Complete each analogy and explain your answer.

1 ☆ + ☆ + ☆ + ☆ : ☆ × 4 :: ♡ + ♡ + ♡ + ♡ + ♡ : _____

How do you know? _____

2 152 ◯ 512 : < :: 541 ◯ 415 : _____

How do you know? _____

3 $3.45 + $1.58 : $5.03 :: $4.23 + $2.99 : _____

How do you know? _____

4 4 + 5 × 6 : 34 :: 3 + 4 × 8 : _____

How do you know? _____

5 $5.00 – $1.30 : $3.70 :: $10.00 – $8.55 : _____

How do you know? _____

Number and Operations   13   ★ ★ • © Carson-Dellosa

Name _____

Date _____

Complete each analogy and explain your answer.

1 52 + 18 + 9 : 50 + 20 + 10 :: 14 + 21 + 39 : _____

_____

How do you know? _____

2 $\frac{2}{4}$: $\frac{1}{2}$ :: $\frac{2}{8}$: _____

_____

How do you know? _____

3 : 12 ÷ 4 :: ⬡⬡ ⬡⬡ ⬡⬡ : _____

_____

How do you know? _____

4 2 shirts at $8.95 each : $17.90 :: 2 pairs of shoes at $12.75 each : _____

_____

How do you know? _____

5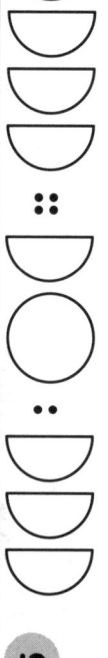

_____

How do you know? _____

Name _____ Date _____

Complete each analogy and explain your answer.

1    ::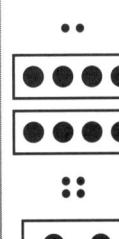

How do you know? _____

2   9,889 < 9,988 : hundreds :: 6,996 > 6,969 :

How do you know? _____

3    : $\frac{10}{7}$ :: 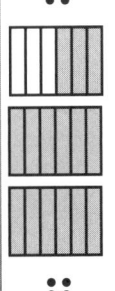 :

How do you know? _____

4 $\frac{1}{4} + \frac{1}{4}$: $\frac{1+1}{4} = \frac{1}{2}$ :: $\frac{2}{8} + \frac{1}{4}$:

How do you know? _____

5 $\frac{5}{100}$: nickel :: $\frac{10}{100}$:

How do you know? _____

Number and Operations

Name _____

Date _____

Complete each analogy and explain your answer.

1   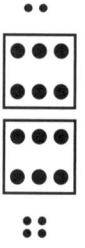 : $1\frac{1}{2}$ ::  :

_____

How do you know? _____

2   change from $10.00 for a bill of $6.25 : 3 dollars and 3 quarters :: change from $20.00 for a bill of $12.95 :

_____

How do you know? _____

3   :: :: :

_____

How do you know? _____

4   4 + 8 = 12 : true :: 12 + 4 = 8 :

_____

How do you know? _____

5   quarter : $\frac{25}{100}$ :: dollar :

_____

How do you know? _____

Number and Operations   16

Name _____

Date _____

Complete each analogy and explain your answer.

1

0 1 2 3 4 5 6 7 8 9 10 11 12 13 14 15 : skip count by 3s :: 12 13 14 15 16 17 18 19 20 21 22 23 24 25 26 27 28 29 30 31 32 : _____

How do you know? _____

2   200 × 50 : 4 zeros :: 8,000 × 50 : _____

How do you know? _____

3   397 × 3 : (400 × 3) – (3 × 3) :: 196 × 5 : _____

How do you know? _____

4

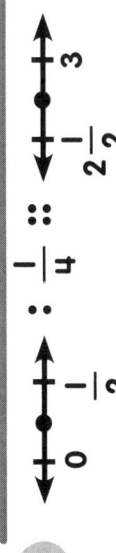

$\frac{1}{2}$: $\frac{1}{4}$ :: $2\frac{1}{2}$:   3   : _____

0    $\frac{1}{2}$ $\frac{1}{4}$ $2\frac{1}{2}$ 3

How do you know? _____

5   475,674 ≈ 480,000 : nearest ten thousand :: 4,756.47 ≈ 4,756.50 : _____

How do you know? _____

Name _____

Complete each analogy and explain your answer.

1. 4 × (3 + ☐) = 40 : 7 :: ☐ + 28 = 40 : _____

    How do you know? _____

2. 2 × (7 + 8) = 56 : false :: 2 × (20 + 8) = 56 : _____

    How do you know? _____

3. $1\frac{25}{100}$: $1.25 :: $2\frac{50}{100}$: _____

    How do you know? _____

4. $\frac{2}{7}$, $\frac{5}{7}$, $\frac{6}{7}$: least to greatest :: $\frac{2}{7}$, $\frac{4}{14}$, $\frac{8}{28}$: _____

    How do you know? _____

5. 4,810 × 4 : (4,000 × 4) + (800 × 4) + (10 × 4) :: 2,307 × 5 : _____

    How do you know? _____

Name _____ Date _____

Complete each analogy and explain your answer.

1  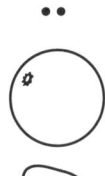 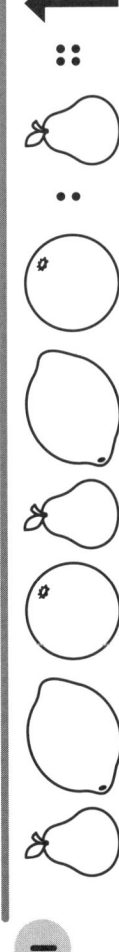 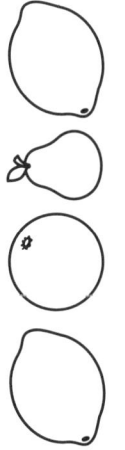 :  ::  : _____

How do you know? _____

2 ABCXABCYABCXABC _____ : Y :: 129312831293I2 _____ :

How do you know? _____

3 3 ↑ $\boxed{+ II}$: 14 :: 18 ↑ $\boxed{+ 23}$: _____

How do you know? _____

4 48 +  = 212 :  ::  + 165 = 329 : _____

How do you know? _____

5 4 + (3 + 8) : (4 + 3) + 8 :: 19 + (7 + 4) : _____

How do you know? _____

Name _____

Complete each analogy and explain your answer.

1 0, 4, 8, 12, _____ : 16 :: 0, 5, 10, 15, _____ : _____

How do you know? _____

2 6 ⟶ ×4 ⟶ 24 :: 8 ⟶ ×7 ⟶ : :

How do you know? _____

3 (6 × 4) × 2 : 6 × (4 × 2) :: (8 × 5) × 7 : _____

How do you know? _____

4 6 ×  = 18 : 3 :: 4 ×  = 20 : _____

How do you know? _____

5 9, 18, 27, _____ : 36 :: 7, 14, 21, _____ : _____

How do you know? _____

Name _____ Date _____

Complete each analogy and explain your answer.

1 2, 4, 7, 11, _____ : 16 :: 5, 7, 10, 14, _____ :

How do you know? _____

2 A, AB, ABC, ABCD, _____ : ABCDE :: K, KL, KLM, KLMN, _____ :

How do you know? _____

3 21, 20, 18, 15, _____ : 11 :: 37, 36, 34, 31, _____ :

How do you know? _____

4 5 →[× 10]→ →[× 100]→ : 50 :: 7 →→ →→ :

How do you know? _____

5 4 × 9 : 9 × 4 :: 8 × 2 :

How do you know? _____

Name _____ Date _____

Complete each analogy and explain your answer.

1 8, 11, 10, 13, 12, _____ : 15 :: 22, 25, 24, 27, 26, _____ :

How do you know? _____

2 120, 60, 30, _____ : 15 :: 80, 40, 20, _____ :

How do you know? _____

3 16 + w : equals 95 :: 24 + w :

How do you know? _____

4 (81 + 75) + 25 [ ] 81 + (75 + 25) : = :: (67 + 54) − 45 [ ] 67 + (54 − 45) :

How do you know? _____

5 ⊙ ⊙ ⊙ ⊙ ⊙ 88 ⊙ ⊙ : ABBC :: ⊙ ⊙ 88 88 ⊙ ⊙ ⊙ 88 88 :

How do you know? _____

Name _____

Date _____

Complete each analogy and explain your answer.

1 5 × y : equals 20 :: 8 × y :

_____

How do you know?

_____

2 16 ÷ 4 ◯ 4 ÷ 16 : ≠ :: 8 × 9 ◯ 9 × 8 :

_____

How do you know?

_____

3 89 – t : equals 65 :: 101 – t :

_____

How do you know?

_____

4 6, 12, 19, _____ : 27 :: 10, 16, 23, _____ :

_____

How do you know?

_____

5 5 lawns mowed each week : $30 :: 8 lawns mowed each week :

_____

How do you know?

_____

 ·

Name _____ Date _____

Complete each analogy and explain your answer.

1 10, 20, 25, 35, 40, _____ : +10, +5 :: 8, 17, 23, 32, 38, _____ : _____

How do you know? _____

_____

2 17 + r + 5 + 13 : equals 41 :: 24 + r + 8 + 12 : _____

How do you know? _____

3 12 hours of TV per week : 96 hours :: 8 hours of TV per week : _____

How do you know? _____

4 🥄🥄🥄🥄 : 20 :: 🥄🥄🥄🥄🥄🥄 : _____

How do you know? _____

5 6 → ☐ → 36 : ×6 :: 9 → ☐ → 72 : _____

How do you know? _____

Name _____

Date _____

Complete each analogy and explain your answer.

1  : 12 :: 🖍🖍🖍🖍🖍 : _____

How do you know? _____

2 25, 50, 100, _____, _____ : 200 :: 20, 60, 180, _____ : _____

How do you know? _____

3 11 pennies in each cup : 88 cents :: 7 pennies in each cup : _____

How do you know? _____

4 5 x 2 x r : 30 :: 2 x 4 x r : _____

How do you know? _____

5 7, 9, 18, 20, 40 : +2, x2 :: 3, 6, 18, 21, 63 : _____

How do you know? _____

Algebra

25

Name _____

Date _____

Complete each analogy and explain your answer.

1 4, 7, 10, . . . : 16 :: 8, 12, 16, . . . : ____

How do you know? _____

2  +  : 2c + 1g = 4c :: 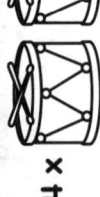 + 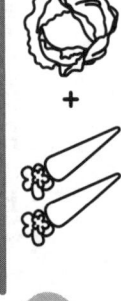 : ____

How do you know? _____

3  : 4 × 2d = 16 :: 5 ×  : ____

4 ×  ____

How do you know? _____

4 7 +  > 8 :  > 1 :: 26 +  < 50 : ____

How do you know? _____

5 87 + n : 93 :: 14 × n : ____

How do you know? _____

Name _____ Date _____

Complete each analogy and explain your answer.

1. 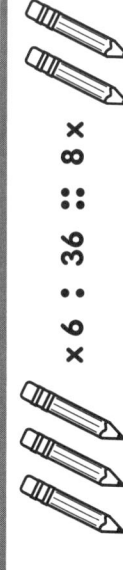 × 6 : 36 :: 8 ×  : _____

How do you know? _____

2. 3, 7, 11, ... : 23 :: 11, 16, 21, ... : _____

How do you know? _____

3. (3 bugs) + (1 bug) : 3f + 1b = 6f :: (2 bugs) + (1 bug) : _____

How do you know? _____

4. 12 × n = 144 : 144 ÷ 12 = n :: 15 × m = 225 : _____

How do you know? _____

5. (moon, star, moon, moon) : ABCA :: (star, moon, moon, moon, star, moon, moon, moon) : _____

How do you know? _____

Name _____

Date _____

Complete each analogy and explain your answer.

1. 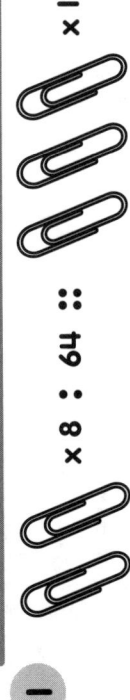 x 8 : 64 ::  x 12 : _____

How do you know? _____

2.  x 6 : 54 ::  x 10 : _____

How do you know? _____

3. GHHAGHHB : 78817882 :: BCBBCDBCBBCE : _____

How do you know? _____

4.  x  : _____ ::  x 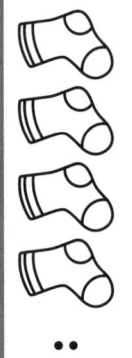 : _____

How do you know? _____

5. 15 : 5 :: 8 : _____

How do you know? _____

Name _____ Date _____

Complete each analogy and explain your answer.

1 7, 10, 13, 16, . . . : 25 :: 12, 16, 20, 24, ... : _____

How do you know? _____

2 5 + 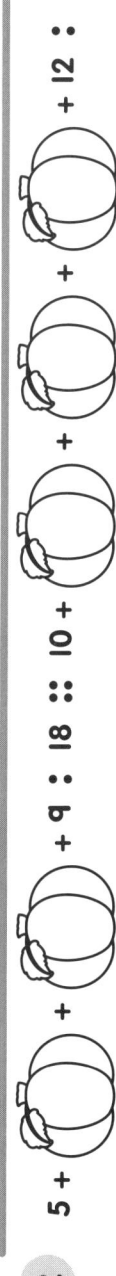 + 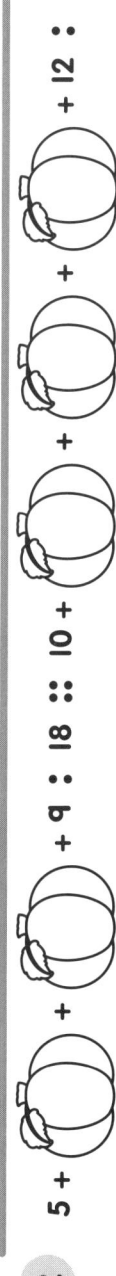 + 9 : 18 :: 10 + 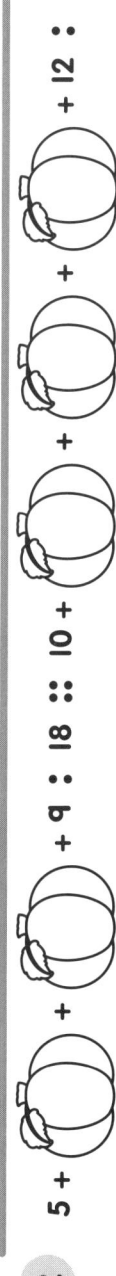 + 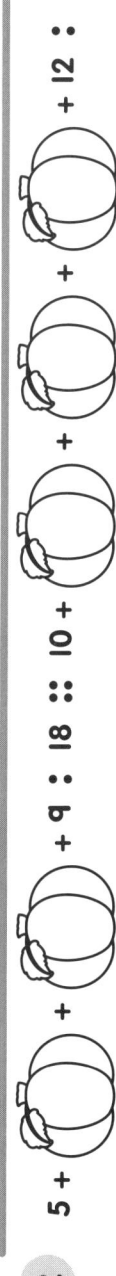 + 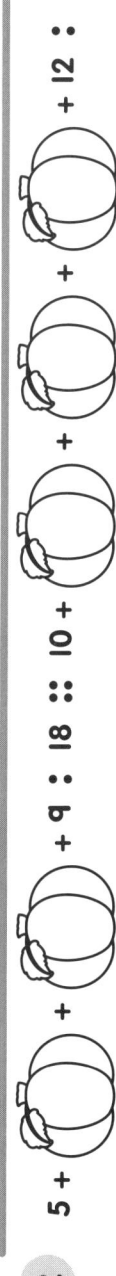 + 12 : _____

How do you know? _____

3  : 10 :: 28 : _____

How do you know? _____

4 14d + 3 : 31 :: 13d + 5 : _____

How do you know? _____

5 6n + 4 : 46 :: 9n + 7 : _____

How do you know? _____

Name _____ Date _____

Complete each analogy and explain your answer.

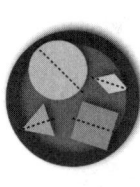

1. ⬠ : trapezoid :: ⬡ : _____

How do you know? _____

2. hexagon : ⬡ :: pentagon : _____

How do you know? _____

3. ▭ : cylinder :: △ : _____

How do you know? _____

4. △△ : similar :: △ △ △ : _____

How do you know? _____

5. obtuse : _____ :: acute : _____

How do you know? _____

Name _____

Date _____

Complete each analogy and explain your answer.

1 ray : •——→ :: line : _____

How do you know? _____

2 _____ : intersecting ::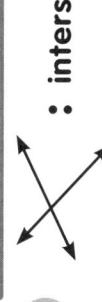

How do you know? _____

3 4 equal sides : square :: 3 equal sides : _____

How do you know? _____

4 octagon : 8 sides :: quadrilateral : _____

How do you know? _____

5 hexa- : 6 :: penta- : _____

How do you know? _____

Name _____ Date _____

Complete each analogy and explain your answer.

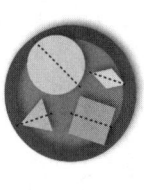

1. :: _____

   How do you know? _____

2. ⬡ :: reflection :: _____

   How do you know? _____

3. 45° : acute angle :: 90° : _____

   How do you know? _____

4. similar : ◯◯ :: congruent : _____

   How do you know? _____

5.  : right triangle :: _____

   How do you know? _____

Name _____   Date _____

Complete each analogy and explain your answer.

1.  + 2 : pentagon :: ☐ + 4 : _____

_____

How do you know? _____

2.  : parallel :: _____

_____

How do you know? _____

3.  : rectangular pyramid :: _____

_____

How do you know? _____

4. acute : < 90° :: obtuse : _____

_____

How do you know? _____

5.  : rotation :: _____

_____

How do you know? _____

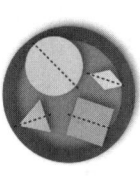

Name _____ Date _____

Complete each analogy and explain your answer.

1. △ ○ ⬠ ⬡ : odd :: □ ⬡ ⯃ : _____

How do you know? _____

2. ⬡ – 2 : quadrilateral :: ⯃ – 5 : _____

How do you know? _____

3. square : right angles :: equilateral triangle : _____

How do you know? _____

4. ⯃ : cube :: ⯃ : _____

How do you know? _____

5. make △ into □ : 3 + 1 :: make ⬠ into ⯃ : _____

How do you know? _____

Geometry

34

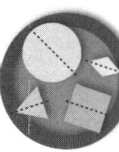

Name _____   Date _____

Complete each analogy and explain your answer.

1.  : (2,3) :: 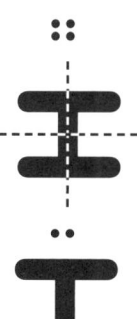 : __

How do you know? _____

2. 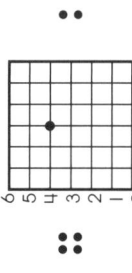 : 6 :: 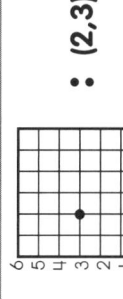 : __

How do you know? _____

3. 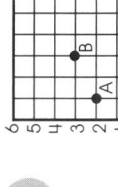 : from point A to point B: right 2, up 1 :: 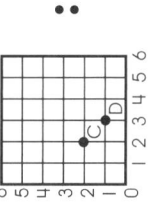 : __

How do you know? _____

4. H :: H :: 8 : __

How do you know? _____

5.  : squares :: 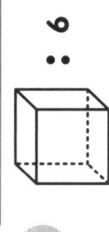 : __

How do you know? _____

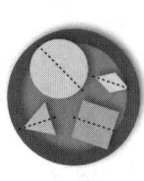

Name _____

Date _____

Complete each analogy and explain your answer.

1 ◯ : not a polygon :: 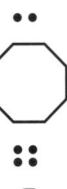 : _____

How do you know? _____

2 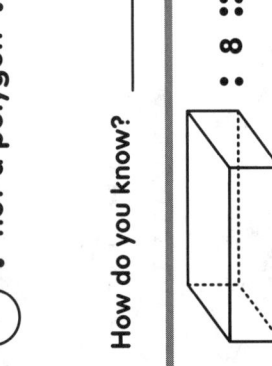 : 8 :: [rectangular prism] : _____

How do you know? _____

3 vertical to horizontal : rotation :: mirror image : _____

How do you know? _____

4 3 triangles inside a pentagon :  :: 4 triangles inside a hexagon : _____

How do you know? _____

5  : 4 blocks :: [blocks] : _____

How do you know? _____

Geometry

Name _____   Date _____

Complete each analogy and explain your answer.

1   5 triangles inside a heptagon :  :: 6 triangles inside an octagon : _____

How do you know? _____

2    : rectangular prism and square pyramid ::  : _____

How do you know? _____

3    - △ + □ : 9 :: □ - □ + △ : _____

How do you know? _____

4   parallelogram : rectangle :: rhombus : _____

How do you know? _____

5   cube : 12 :: square pyramid : _____

How do you know? _____

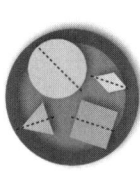

Name _____ Date _____

Complete each analogy and explain your answer.

1 (1,2) (1,4) : vertical line :: (4,3) (6,3) : _____

How do you know? _____

2  L : ⌐ :: B : _____

How do you know? _____

3 > < V : reflection, rotation ::  : _____

How do you know? _____

4 octagon, hexagon, triangle : greatest to least :: acute angle, right angle, obtuse angle : _____

How do you know? _____

5 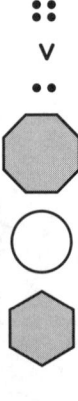 :: < ::  : _____

How do you know? _____

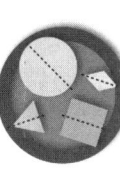

Name _____   Date _____

Complete each analogy and explain your answer.

1 triangle : pentagon :: square : _____

How do you know? _____

2 line segment : 2 :: ray : _____

How do you know? _____

3  : will intersect :: _____

How do you know? _____

4 right triangle : 1 :: square : _____

How do you know? _____

5 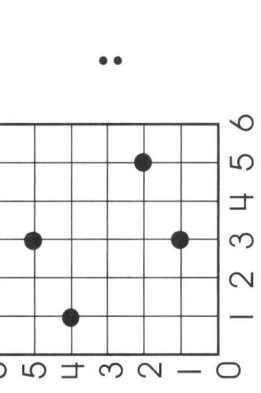 : triangle :: 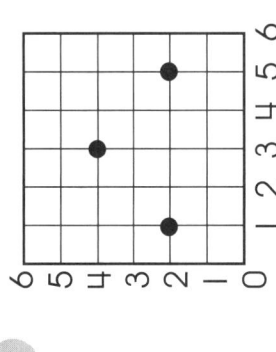 : _____

How do you know? _____

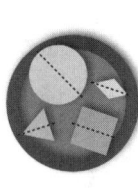

Name _____

Date _____

Complete each analogy and explain your answer.

1 53°, 53°, 74° : isosceles :: 85°, 43°, 52° : _____

How do you know? _____

2 (0,4) (1,1) (2,5) (3,1) (4,4) : pentagon :: (1,1) (1,3) (3,1) (3,3) : _____

How do you know? _____

3 parallelogram with 1 hexagon and 2 triangles :  :: trapezoid with 1 hexagon and 2 triangles : _____

How do you know? _____

4  : true :: _____

How do you know? _____

5 (1,1) (1,4) (2,1) (2,4) moved to (3,1) (3,4) (4,1) (4,4) : translation :: (1,1) (2,2) (3,1) moved to (1,4) (2,3) (3,4) : _____

How do you know? _____

★★★ •

Complete each analogy and explain your answer.

1 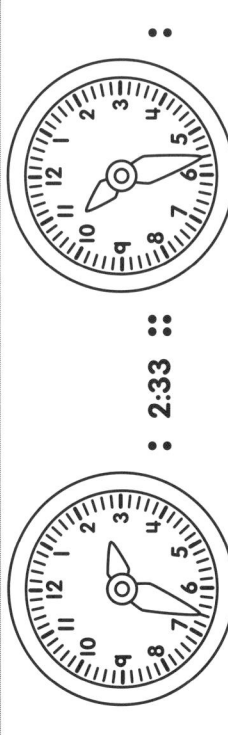 : 2:33 :: _____ :

How do you know? _____

2 kilometer : km :: centimeter : _____

How do you know? _____

3  : 6.5 cm :: _____ :

How do you know? _____

4 20 meters : 2,000 centimeters :: 15 meters : _____

How do you know? _____

5 4 yards : 12 feet :: 12 yards : _____

How do you know? _____

Name _____

Date _____

Complete each analogy and explain your answer.

1 **8 pints : 4 quarts :: 16 pints :** _____

How do you know? _____

2 **June : 30 :: October :** _____

How do you know? _____

3 **5:15 P.M. to 6:10 P.M. : 55 minutes :: 4:35 P.M. to 5:05 P.M. :** _____

How do you know? _____

4

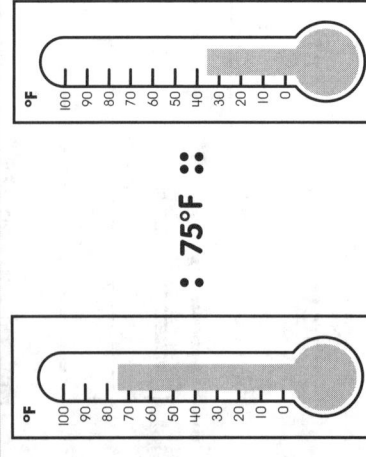

: 75°F :: _____ **:** _____

How do you know? _____

5 **1 lb. : 16 oz. :: 1 kg :** _____

How do you know? _____

Name _____ Date _____

Complete each analogy and explain your answer.

1 212°F : water boils :: 32°F : _____

How do you know? _____

2 60 inches : 5 feet :: 84 inches : _____

How do you know? _____

3  12:35 to 4:15 : 3 hours, 40 minutes ::  6:15 to 11:50 : _____

How do you know? _____

4 48 hours : 2 days :: 72 hours : _____

How do you know? _____

5 200 cm : 2 m :: 800 cm : _____

How do you know? _____

Measurement

43

Name _____

Complete each analogy and explain your answer.

1 $1\frac{1}{2}$ feet : 1 foot, 6 inches :: $1\frac{1}{2}$ meters : _____

_____

How do you know? _____

2 grams : ounces :: kilograms : _____

_____

How do you know? _____

3 1 pint + 1 cup : 3 cups :: 1 quart + 1 cup : _____

_____

How do you know? _____

4 _____ : freezing point of water :: 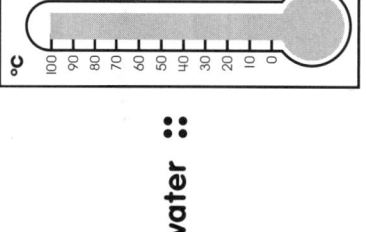 :

_____

How do you know? _____

5 52 weeks : 1 year :: 156 weeks : _____

_____

How do you know? _____

Name _____

Date _____

Complete each analogy and explain your answer.

1 10 quarts ◯ 3 gallons : < :: 18 quarts ◯ 4 gallons :

_____

How do you know? _____

2 school bus : meters :: paper clip :

_____

How do you know? _____

3 21 days : 3 weeks :: 42 days :

_____

How do you know? _____

4 3 pints – 2 cups : 4 cups :: 5 pints – 4 cups :

_____

How do you know? _____

5

2 in. : 12 in. ::

4 in.

4 in. ::

8 in.

_____

How do you know? _____

Measurement

45

★★ · © Carson-Dellosa

Name _____

Date _____

Complete each analogy and explain your answer.

1 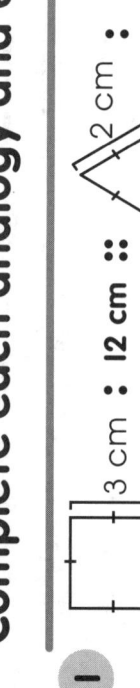 3 cm : 12 cm :: 2 cm : ____ :

How do you know? _____

2 glass of water : cup :: swimming pool : ____

How do you know? _____

3 five half hours : $2\frac{1}{2}$ hours :: six quarter hours : ____

How do you know? _____

4  : 21 square units :: 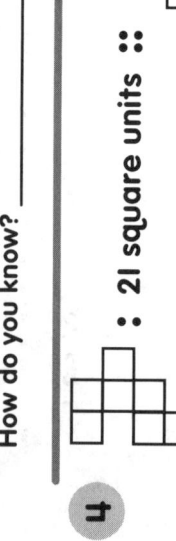 : ____

How do you know? _____

5 kilometer : 1,000 meters :: kilo : ____

How do you know? _____

Measurement

46

Name _____ Date _____

Complete each analogy and explain your answer.

1 $\frac{1}{2}$ mile : 2,640 feet :: $\frac{1}{4}$ mile : _____

How do you know? _____

2 2 liters of water each day per week : about 4 pints :: 4 liters of water each day per week : _____

How do you know? _____

3 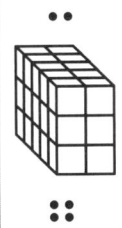 : 32 cubic units :: 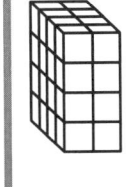 : _____

How do you know? _____

4 90 seconds : 1 $\frac{1}{2}$ minutes :: 150 seconds : _____

How do you know? _____

5 2 cups cat food each day per week : 7 pints :: 4 cups dog food each day per week : _____

How do you know? _____

Name _____

Date _____

Complete each analogy and explain your answer.

1 32°F : 0°C :: 212°F : _____

How do you know? _____

2 4,000 m for 5 days : 20 km :: 2,000 m for 8 days : _____

How do you know? _____

3 North Carolina to California : mi. :: pencil eraser to point : _____

4  :  $\frac{1}{4}$ ::  :

How do you know? _____

5 9 in. : 66 in. :: 2 ft. 6 in. : 3 ft. _____

How do you know? _____

Measurement   48

★★★ · © Carson-Dellosa

Name _____ Date _____

Complete each analogy and explain your answer.

1 three quarts lemonade **:** six pints **::** seven quarts lemonade **:** _____

How do you know? _____

2 12 **:** ruler **::** 36 **:** _____

How do you know? _____

3 14th **:** Saturday **::** 23rd **:** _____

How do you know? _____

4 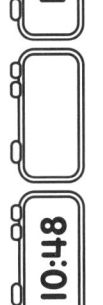 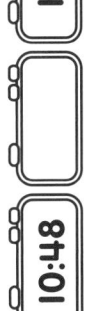   **::**

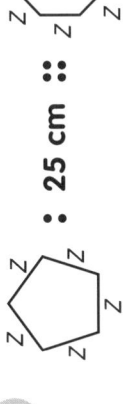 10:48 [ ] 1:20 2:36 **::**

How do you know? _____

5 [pentagon labeled n, n, n, n, n] **:** 25 cm **::** [octagon labeled n, n, n, n, n, n, n, n] **:** _____

How do you know? _____

Name _____

Complete each analogy and explain your answer.

1 this Monday : March 29th :: next Monday : _____

How do you know? _____

2 6 cups of juice per day : 21 pints :: 2 cups of juice per day : _____

How do you know? _____

3 January through June : about $\frac{1}{2}$ :: January through September : _____

How do you know? _____

4 deci- ◯ milli- : > :: centi- ◯ kilo- : _____

How do you know? _____

5

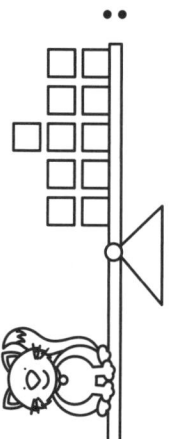

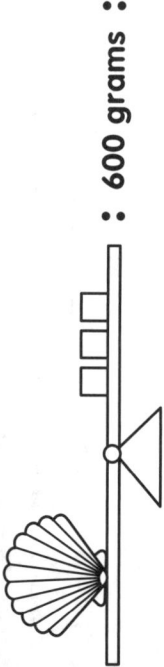

_____ : 600 grams :: _____ :

How do you know? _____

Name _____

Date _____

Complete each analogy and explain your answer.

1   40 min. : $\frac{2}{3}$ :: 1 hr. 20 min. : _____

How do you know? _____

2   centimeter : meter :: penny : _____

How do you know? _____

3   plane figure : area :: solid figure : _____

How do you know? _____

4

How do you know? _____

5   1 x 5 : 30 square miles :: 1 + 1 + 5 + 5 : _____

How do you know? _____

Name _____

Date _____

Complete each analogy and explain your answer.

1 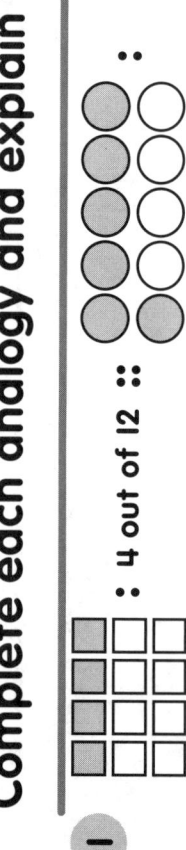 :: 4 out of 12 ::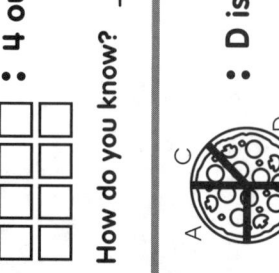

How do you know?

_____

2  :: D is the largest. ::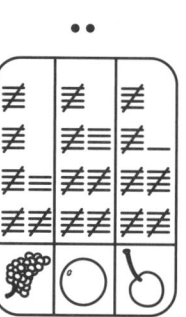

How do you know?

_____

3 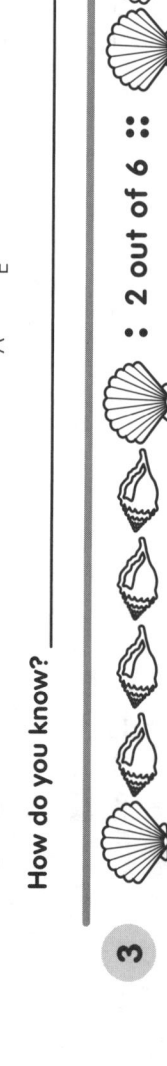 :: 2 out of 6 ::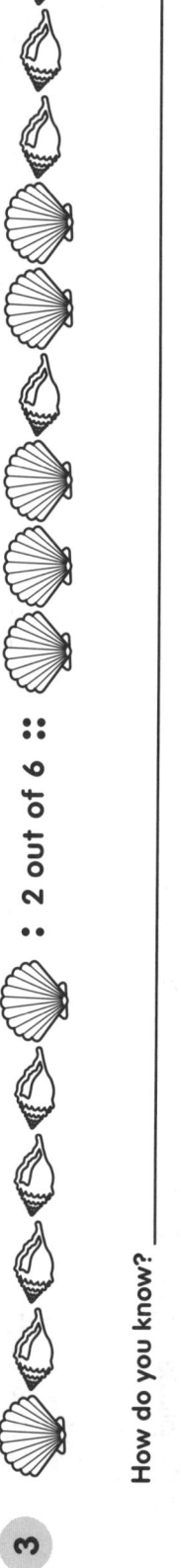

How do you know?

_____

4  :: White is most likely. ::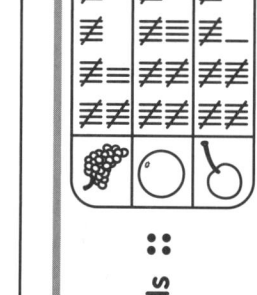

How do you know?

_____

5 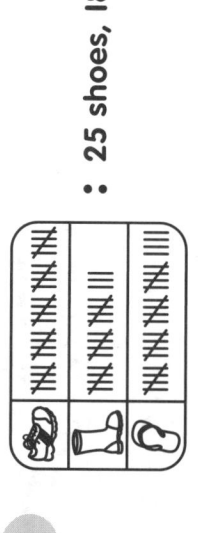 :: 25 shoes, 18 boots, 24 sandals ::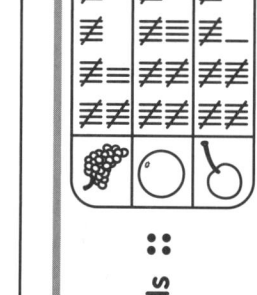

How do you know?

_____

Name _____ Date _____

Complete each analogy and explain your answer.

1

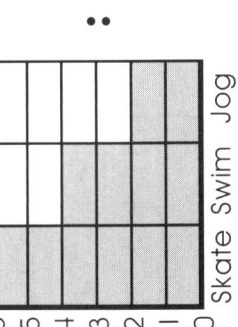
6
5
4
3
2
1
0
Walk Bike Drive

: Bike is the most popular. **::**

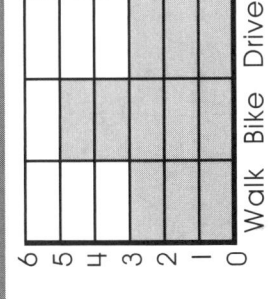
6
5
4
3
2
1
0
Skate Swim Jog

: _____

How do you know? _____

2

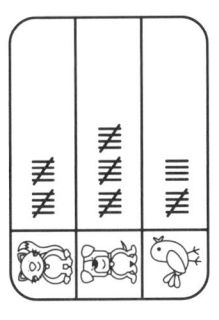

: Dogs are the fewest. **::**

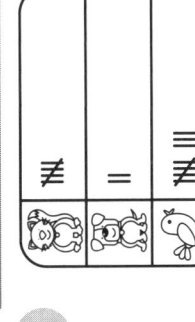

: _____

How do you know? _____

3

October : $\dfrac{1}{12}$ **::** Monday : _____

How do you know? _____

4

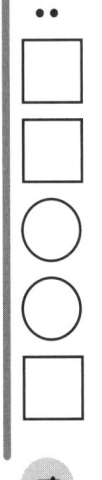 : $\dfrac{2}{5}$ **::** _____ : _____

How do you know? _____

5

purple, white, yellow : purple & white, purple & yellow, white & yellow **::** black, red, green : _____

How do you know? _____

Name _____ Date _____

Complete each analogy and explain your answer.

1.

```
        X
  X  X  X              X  X
  X  X  X  X        X   X  X
 +--+--+--+--+    +--+--+--+--+--+--+--+
 5  10 15 20 25 30   10 20 30 40 50 60 70
```

: range = 15 :: :

How do you know? _____

2.

pizza	卌 卌 IIII
chicken	卌 卌 III
burger	卌 卌 II

: Burger is the least popular. ::

pear	卌 卌 III
apple	卌 卌 IIII
orange	卌 卌 卌

:

How do you know? _____

3. range of (8, 7, 10, 15, 5, 4) : 15 − 4 = 11 :: range of (17, 12, 6, 3, 1, 8) :

How do you know? _____

4. You will choose a red marble from a bag of 0 purple and 10 red. : certain :: You will choose a yellow marble from a bag of 25 orange and 0 yellow. :

How do you know? _____

5.

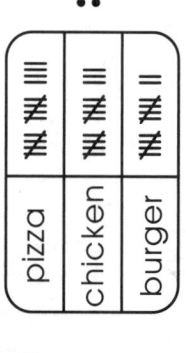

March	☀☀☀☀
April	☀☀
May	☀☀☀☀☀

☀ = 4 sunny days

: May ::

December	❄❄❄
January	❄❄❄❄❄❄
February	❄❄❄❄❄

❄ = 2 snowy days

:

How do you know? _____

Name _____

Date _____

Complete each analogy and explain your answer.

1 R, R, S, T, S, T, R : $\frac{3}{7}$ :: A, B, R, B, R, A, B, R, R : _____

How do you know? _____

2 I out of 5 : unlikely :: 9 out of 10 : _____

How do you know? _____

3 red, blue, yellow : 3 pair combinations :: green, blue, purple, white : _____

How do you know? _____

4

purple	卌
green	III
yellow	II

probability of blue : impossible ::

red	I
blue	卌 I
orange	卌 卌

probability of red : _____

How do you know? _____

5 A person will be famous. : not likely :: A person will learn to drive. : _____

How do you know? _____

Data Analysis and Probability

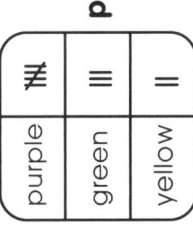 · © Carson-Dellosa

Name _____

Complete each analogy and explain your answer.

1 tossing a coin : $\frac{1}{2}$ :: rolling a die : _____

How do you know? _____

2

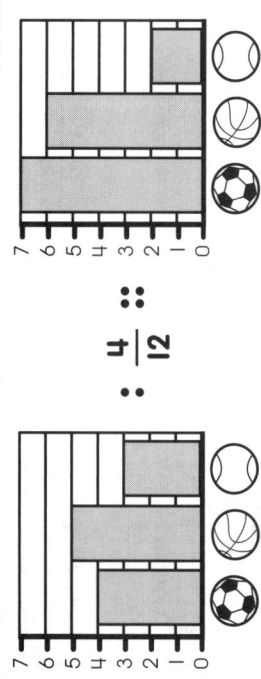

$\frac{4}{12}$ ::   : _____

How do you know? _____

3

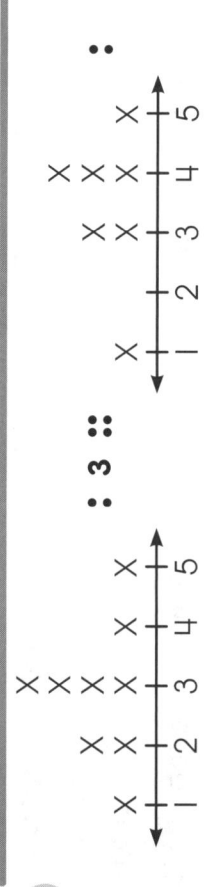

: 3 ::   : _____

How do you know? _____

4 blue when $\frac{1}{8}$ red, $\frac{1}{8}$ yellow, $\frac{3}{4}$ blue : most likely :: red when $\frac{1}{20}$ red, $\frac{1}{5}$ purple, $\frac{1}{4}$ blue, $\frac{1}{2}$ orange : _____

How do you know? _____

5 22, 65, 89, 34, 65, 33 : 65 :: 45, 77, 96, 56, 77, 33 : _____

How do you know? _____

Name _____

Date _____

Complete each analogy and explain your answer.

1 X, Y, Z : XY, XZ, YZ :: A, B, C, D : _____

How do you know? _____

2 1,025 1,000 1,050 1,010 1,500 : 1,025 :: 8,008 8,018 8,000 8,800 8,080 : _____

How do you know? _____

3 red, red, blue, white, red, blue : red :: orange, green, purple, green, blue : _____

How do you know? _____

4 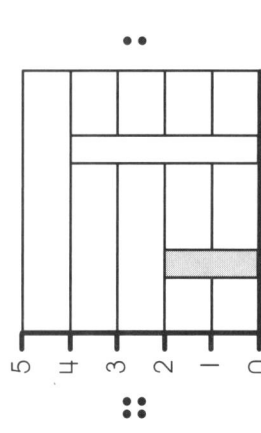 :: greatest :: _____

How do you know? _____

5 Titans = 18 games won : ◯ ◯ ◯ ◯ ◯ ◖ :: Knights = 10 games won : _____

How do you know? _____

Name _____

Date _____

Complete each analogy and explain your answer.

1   25, 14, 6, 8, 23 : 19 :: 41, 18, 9, 2, 1 : _____

How do you know? _____

2   red shirt, yellow shirt, blue pants, white pants : RS & BP, RS & WP, YS & BP, YS & WP :: orange shirt, black shirt, green pants, brown pants : _____

How do you know? _____

3   4 chess players play each other only once : 6 games :: 5 chess players play each other only once : _____

How do you know? _____

4   980, 989, 988, 879, 987 : 987 :: 636, 635, 653, 665, 356 : _____

How do you know? _____

5   (graph, temperature decreasing over time of day) : increasing :: (graph, temperature increasing over time of day) : _____

How do you know? _____

Name _____ Date _____

Complete each analogy and explain your answer.

1   2,295 2,287 2,296 2,300 : 13 :: 2,285 2,286 2,280 2,280 2,299 :

How do you know? _____

2   range of (a, a, b, c, d, d, d) : d – a :: mode of (a, a, b, c, d, d, d) :

How do you know? _____

3   6 people shake each other's hands once : 15 handshakes :: 8 people shake each other's hands once :

How do you know? _____

4
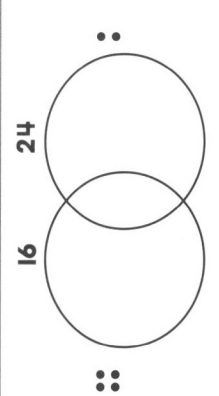
: 20 ::
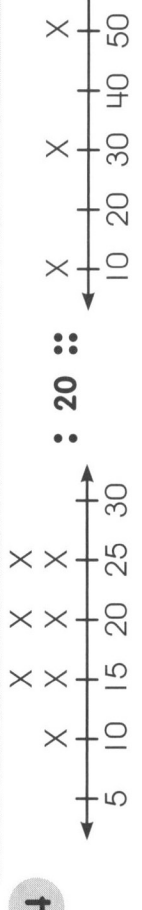
:

How do you know? _____

5
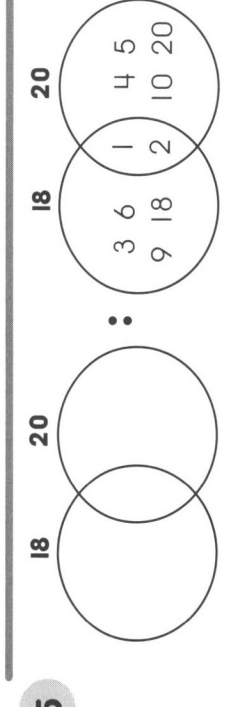

How do you know? _____

Name _____   Date _____

Complete each analogy and explain your answer.

1 12, 13, 15, 16 : 14 :: 16, 17, 21, 22 : _____

How do you know? _____

2

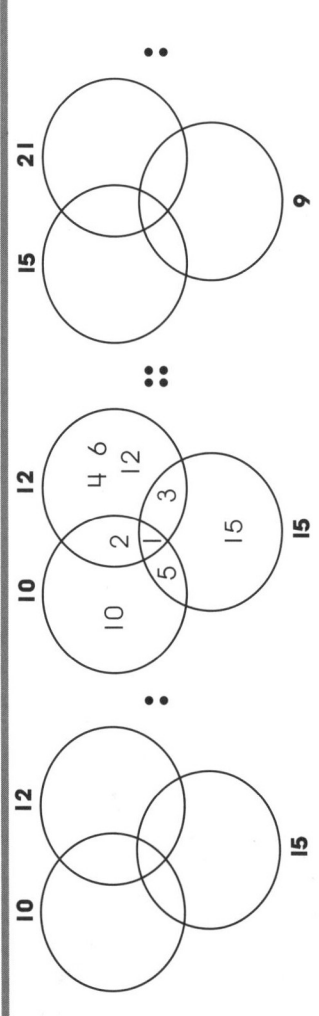

10   12   10   12   15   21

          10   4 6
               2   12
             5 1 3
               15   9

15   15

How do you know? _____

3 red shirt, purple shirt, blue pants, green pants, white belt, orange belt : RBW, RBO, RGW, RGO, PBW, PBO, PGW, PGO :: yellow coat, black coat, pink scarf, green scarf, violet mittens, white mittens : _____

How do you know? _____

4

A	卌 卌
B	卌
C	卌

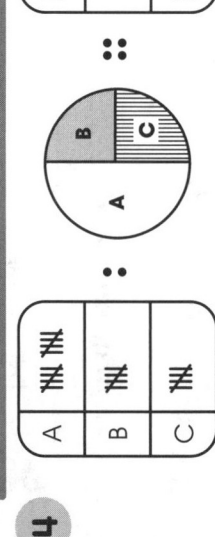

A   B   C

D	|||
E	卌 |||
F	|||

How do you know? _____

5 98, 96, 95, 93, 92, 97, 94 : 95 :: 85, 86, 82, 83, 81, 84, 80 : _____

How do you know? _____

Answer Key

Note: There may be more than one correct answer for each analogy. Use judgement when evaluating a student's answers.

Page 6
1. seven hundreds; Write the number of hundreds in words. 2. 2,000; Round to the nearest thousand. 3. greatest to least; Describe the order of the values. 4. 825; Regroup the tens and write the number. 5. eight hundred forty-three; Write the number in words.

Page 7
1. $\frac{1}{3}$; Write the fraction that represents the shaded portion of the shape. 2. 8 thousands; Write the number of thousands. 3. 3,522; Write the number word as a number. 4. 50,000; Round to the nearest ten thousand. 5. 3 × 5; Write the repeated addition expression as a multiplication fact.

Page 8
1. 7,000 + 900 + 20 + 4; Write the number in expanded form. 2. ▤ ; Divide a rectangle and shade the fraction described. 3. 6,600; Round to the nearest hundred. 4. $1.50; Add the value of the coins. 5. 80 tens; Write the hundreds as tens.

Page 9
1. 6,051; Write the number in standard form. 2. 1,039; Regroup the tens and write the number described. 3. 10 + 20; Round each number in the expression to the nearest ten. 4. 9 + 9 + 9; Write the multiplication fact as a repeated addition expression. 5. $2.80; Add the value of the coins.

Page 10
1. least to greatest; Describe the order of the values of the fractions pictured. 2. 90; Round to the nearest ten and then add. 3. $\frac{1}{3}$; Write the fraction depicted in the first part of the analogy. 4. 14; Write the Roman numeral as a number in standard form. 5. 6 × 5; Write the corresponding multiplication fact for the division fact.

Page 11
1. 18,000; Multiply. 2. $1\frac{1}{2}$; Add the fractions and write the sum as a mixed number. 3. 60; Multiply by 12 to write the total number. 4. IV; Subtract the Roman numerals. 5. 19; Using the order of operations, multiply first and then add.

Page 12
1. 36 ÷ 6; Write the corresponding division fact for the multiplication fact. 2. least to greatest; Describe the order of the values. 3. 5,200; Round each number to the nearest hundred and add. 4. multiply; Name the operation that will make the number sentence true. 5. 4,500; Multiply.

Page 13
1. ♥ × 5; Write the multiplication expression to match the repeated addition. 2. >; Write the symbol to compare the numbers. 3. $7.22; Add and write the sum. 4. 35; Using the order of operations, multiply first and then add. 5. $1.45; Subtract and write the difference.

Page 14
1. 10 + 20 + 40; Round each number to the nearest ten. 2. $\frac{1}{4}$; Write the fraction in lowest terms. 3. 8 ÷ 2; Write the division expression that matches the picture. 4. $25.50; Add the amount twice or multiply by 2. 5. ◯◯◖ ; Combine the halves into a depiction of the equivalent mixed number.

Page 15
1. ⚃⚃⚃⚃ ; Use the commutative property of multiplication to illustrate the multiplication fact. 2. tens; Write the place value position that helps you decide whether the number is greater than or less than. 3. $\frac{15}{6}$; Write the mixed number shown. 4. $\frac{1}{2}$; Add the fractions and write the sum in lowest terms. 5. dime; Write the name of the coin whose value is expressed by the fraction.

Page 16
1. $4\frac{1}{2}$; Write the mixed number that corresponds to the dot on the number line. 2. 7 dollars and 1 nickel; Subtract and describe the change. 3. ⚄⚄⚄⚄⚄ ; Use the commutative property of multiplication to illustrate the multiplication fact. 4. false; Write whether the rearrangement of numbers in the addition problem still gives you a true sentence. 5. $\frac{100}{100}$ or 1; Write the fraction that expresses the value of the money.

Page 17
1. skip count by 4s; Describe the addition facts represented by the number line. 2. 5 zeros; Write the number of zeros in the product. 3. (200 × 5) − (4 × 5); Round 397 up. Multiply the difference (3) between the rounded number and the original number by the smaller factor

and subtract. 4. $2\frac{3}{4}$; Write the mixed number that corresponds to the dot on the number line. 5. nearest tenth; Write the place to which the number was rounded.

Page 18
1. 12; Write the missing number from the number sentence. 2. true; Determine whether the number sentence is true or false. 3. $2.50; Write the amount of money expressed by the fraction. 4. equivalent fractions; Write the relation of the fractions. 5. (2,000 × 5) + (300 × 5) + (7 × 5); Write in expanded form using the distributive property.

Page 19
1. ↑; Draw the next symbol in the repeating pattern. 2. 8; Write the next number in the repeating pattern. 3. 41; Apply the function to the original number. 4. 🐚 = 164; Find the value of the variable. 5. (19 + 7) + 4; Use the associative property of addition to regroup the addends.

Page 20
1. 20; Write the next number in the growing pattern. 2. 56; Apply the function to the original number. 3. 8 × (5 × 7); Use the associative property of multiplication to regroup the factors. 4. 5; Find the value of the variable. 5. 28; Write the next number in the growing pattern.

Page 21
1. 19; Write the next number in the growing (+2, +3, +4, . . .) pattern. 2. KLMNO; Write the next letter in the growing (+1) pattern. 3. 27; Write the next letter in the shrinking (−1, −2, −3, . . .) pattern. 4. 700; Apply the function to the original number. 5. 2 × 8; Use the commutative property of multiplication to rearrange the factors.

Page 22
1. 29; Write the next number in the (+3, −1) pattern. 2. 10; Divide by 2 and write the next number. 3. equals 103; Solve for w in the first part of the analogy (95 − 16 = 79). Then, substitute 79 for w in the second part of the analogy and add to solve. 4. =; Determine whether the two expressions are equal. 5. AABCC; Translate the repeating section of the pattern into letters.

Page 23

1. equals 32; Solve for y in the first part of the analogy ($20 \div 5 = 4$). Then, substitute 4 for y in the second part of the analogy and multiply to solve. 2. =; Determine whether the two expressions are equal. 3. equals 77; Solve for t in the first part of the analogy ($89 - 65 = 24$). Then, substitute 24 for t in the second part of the analogy and subtract to solve. 4. 31; Write the next number in the growing (+6, +7, . . .) pattern. 5. \$48; The first part of the analogy tells \$6 was made from mowing each lawn, because 5 × \$6 = \$30. So, multiply 8 lawns times \$6.

Page 24

1. +9, +6; Write the rule for the pattern. 2. equals 50; Solve for r in the first part of the analogy ($41 - 35 = 6$). Then, substitute 6 for r in the second part of the analogy and add to solve. 3. 64 hours; The first part of the analogy tells that 8 weeks of TV are being watched because $12 \times 8 = 96$. So, multiply 8 hours times 8 weeks. 4. 30; Divide 20 by 4 to find the value of each spoon (5). Then, multiply 5 by 6. 5. ×8; Divide 72 by 9 to find the rule for the function.

Page 25

1. 20; Divide 12 by 3 to find the value of each crayon (4). Then, multiply 4×5. 2. 540; Write the next number in the (×3) pattern. 3. 56 cents; The first part of the analogy tells that there are 8 cups because $8 \times 11 = 88$. So, multiply 7 pennies by 8 cups. 4. 24; Solve for r in the first part of the analogy ($30 \div 10 = 3$). Then, substitute 3 for r in the second part of the analogy and multiply to solve. 5. +3, ×3; Write the rule for the pattern.

Page 26

1. 24; Find the number after the next number. 2. $1c + 2g = 5c$; Write the linear function for the picture shown. 3. $5 \times 3d = 30$; Write the linear function for the picture shown. 4.  < 24; Find the value for the variable that makes the inequality true. 5. 84; Solve for n in the first part of the analogy ($93 - 87 = 6$). Then, substitute 6 for n in the second part of the analogy.

Page 27

1. 32; The first part of the analogy tells that each pencil equals 2 because $2 + 2 + 2 = 6$ and $6 \times 6 = 36$. So, multiply 8 by (2 + 2), or 4. 2. 36; Find the third number out in the (+5) pattern. 3. $1f + 1b = 4f$; Write the linear function for the picture shown. 4. $225 \div 15 = m$; Write the corresponding division problem. 5. CCAAB; Translate the pictures into a letter pattern following the same rules as the first part of the analogy.

Page 28

1. 144; The first part of the analogy tells that each paper clip is equal to 4 because $4 + 4 = 8$ and $8 \times 8 = 64$. So, multiply 12 by (4 + 4 + 4), or 12. 2. 60; The first part of the analogy tells that each rake is equal to 3 because $3 + 3 + 3 = 9$ and $9 \times 6 = 54$. So, multiply 10 by (3 + 3), or 6. 3. 232234232235; Translate the letter pattern to the corresponding numbers. 4. ; The first part of the analogy tells that a shoe multiplies the number of socks by 2. So, multiply the 3 socks by 2. 5. 2; Divide the number on the right by the number of pears on the left to find how much each pear must "weigh" to balance the scale.

Page 29

1. 36; Find the third number out in the (+4) pattern. 2. 28; The first part of the analogy tells that each pumpkin is equal to 2 because $2 + 2 = 4$ and $(5 + 4) + 9 = 18$. So, add $[10 + (2 + 2 + 2)] + 12$. 3. 7; Divide the number on the right by the number of apples on the left to find how much each apple must "weigh" to balance the scale. 4. 31; The first part of the analogy tells us that $d = 2$ ($14 \times 2 + 3 = 31$), so substitute 2 for d in the second part of the analogy. 5. 70; The first part of the analogy tells us that $n = 7$ ($6 \times 7 + 4 = 46$), so substitute 7 for n in the second part of the analogy.

Page 30

1. octagon; Write the name of the polygon. 2. ; Draw the polygon named. 3. cone; Write the name of the 3-D figure. 4. congruent; Describe the relationship between the two triangles. 5. 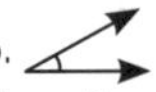; Draw the type of angle described.

Page 31

1. ; Draw the figure described. 2. parallel or not intersecting; Describe the lines. 3. equilateral triangle; Write the name of the polygon described. 4. 4 sides; Write the number of sides for the polygon named. 5. 5; Write the number associated with the prefix.

Page 32

1. ; Draw the reflection of the figure. 2. rotation; Write the name of the transformation applied. 3. right angle; Write the name of the angle described. 4. ; Draw the circles so that they are congruent. 5. isosceles triangle; Write the name of the triangle.

Page 33

1. octagon; Write the name of the polygon that has the same number of sides as a square plus 4. 2. perpendicular; Describe the lines. 3. cube; Write the name of the solid figure that the net can be folded into. 4. > 90°; Describe the angle in terms of degrees. 5. translation; Write the name of the transformation applied.

Page 34

1. even; Describe the number of sides of the polygons as *even* or *odd*. 2. triangle; Write the name of the polygon that has the same number of sides as an octagon minus 5. 3. acute angles; Describe the types of angles in the polygon. 4. rectangular prism; Write the name of the solid figure that the net can be folded into. 5. 5 + 3; Write an addition expression to show how many more sides are needed to change a pentagon to an octagon.

Page 35

1. (3,4); Write the ordered pair for the plotted point. 2. 4; Write the number of faces that the figure has. 3. From point C to point D: right 1, down 1; Describe the path from point A to point B. 4. ; Draw the figure with all lines of symmetry marked. 5. rectangles; Name the shape that the 3-D figure is made of.

Page 36

1. a polygon; Write whether the figure is a polygon. 2. 6; Write the number of vertices that the figure has. 3. reflection; Name the transformation described. 4. ; Draw the figure divided into triangles as described and in the same manner as the first part of the analogy. 5. 15 blocks; Write the number of blocks that are in the figure.

Page 37

1. ; Draw the figure divided into triangles as described and in the same manner as the first part of the analogy. 2. cylinder and cone; Write the names of the solid figures that are combined in the figure. 3. 4; Solve the expression using the number of sides. 4. square; Write the name of the polygon that is a type of rhombus with right angles. 5. 8; Write the number of edges that the solid shape has.

Page 38

1. horizontal line; Write the type of line that the points would be on if plotted. 2. ; Draw the image transformed in the same way as the example (reflection, rotation). 3. translation, reflection; Describe the transformations applied to the shape. 4. least to greatest; Describe the order of the angles based on their degrees. 5. >; The number of sides on a pentagon is greater than the number of sides on a triangle.

Page 39

1. hexagon; Name the polygon that has two more sides than the polygon given. 2. 1; Write the number of points that the figure has. 3. will not intersect; The lines, if continued in the directions shown, will never intersect. 4. 4; Write the number of right angles in the polygon. 5. rectangle; Name the shape that can be formed by connecting the plotted points.

Page 40

1. scalene; Describe the type of triangle with three different angles. 2. square; Name the polygon that would be formed by connecting the points if they were plotted. 3. ; Draw the figure described using the shapes listed. 4. false; The symbols on the cube do not match the placement of the symbols on the net of the cube. 5. reflection; Describe the transformation of the shape made by the points if they were plotted.

Page 41

1. 10:28; Write the time shown on the clock. 2. cm; Write the abbreviation for the metric unit given. 3. 7.5 cm; Measure and write the length of the object in centimeters. 4. 1,500 centimeters; Multiply by 100 to write the equivalent number of centimeters to the number of meters given. 5. 36 feet; Multiply by 3 to write the equivalent number of feet for the number of yards given.

Page 42

1. 8 quarts; Divide by 2 to write the equivalent number of quarts for the number of pints given. 2. 31; Write the number of days in the month. 3. 30 minutes; Write the elapsed time. 4. 35°F; Write the temperature shown on the thermometer. 5. 1,000 g; Write the number of smaller units of metric weight in 1 kg (kilo = 1,000).

Page 43

1. water freezes; Write the critical point described by the temperature. 2. 7 feet; Divide by 12 to write the equivalent number of feet. 3. 5 hours, 35 minutes; Write the elapsed time between the two clocks. 4. 3 days; Write the number of days represented by the number of hours. 5. 8 m; Divide by 100 to write the equivalent number of meters.

Page 44

1. 1 meter, 50 cm; Describe the fractional amount in terms of the next smaller unit. 2. pounds; Write the similar unit of customary measurement. 3. 5 cups; Write the total in terms of the smaller unit of capacity. 4. boiling point of water; Write the critical point described by the temperature shown. 5. 3 years; Convert weeks to years.

Page 45

1. >; Convert gallons to quarts (4 qt. × 4 gal. = 16 qt.) and compare the number of quarts. 2. centimeters; Write the best unit of metric length to use to measure the item. 3. 6 weeks; Convert days to weeks. 4. 6 cups; Write the difference in terms of the smaller unit of capacity. 5. 24 in.; Write the perimeter of the polygon.

Page 46

1. 6 cm; Write the perimeter of the polygon. 2. gallon; Write the best unit of customary capacity to use to measure the item. 3. $1\frac{1}{2}$ hours; Combine the quarter hours and write the total as a mixed number. 4. 36 square units; Use the first part of the analogy to determine that a square is 3 square units (21 ÷ 7 = 3), then apply that to the second figure. 5. 1,000; Write the meaning of the metric prefix.

Page 47

1. 1,320 feet; Halve the number of feet in a half mile. 2. about 8 pints; Use the first part of the analogy to determine that 1 liter is twice as much as 1 pint. Write the number of pints. 3. 30 cubic units; Count the cubes to write the volume of the figure. 4. $2\frac{1}{2}$ minutes; Write the number of minutes that are equal to the number of seconds. 5. 14 pints; Write the number of pints for the number of cups (4 cups × 7 days, or 28 cups).

Page 48

1. 100°C; Write the Celsius equivalent for the Fahrenheit temperature of boiling water. 2. 16 km; Convert meters to kilometers and then multiply by the number of days. 3. in.; Write the best unit of customary length to use to measure the object. 4. $3\frac{1}{4}$; Express the elapsed time as the fraction of the clock covered by the minute hand. 5. 84 in.; Convert feet to inches and find the perimeter.

Page 49

1. 14 pints; Multiply by 2 to convert quarts to pints. 2. yardstick; Write the measuring tool that has that number of units. 3. Monday; Use the date and day in the first part of the analogy to write the day for the date given. 4. 12:04; Write the missing time in the pattern. 5. 40 cm; Solve for z (25 cm ÷ 5 sides, or 5 cm) and multiply by 8 sides to calculate the perimeter of the octagon.

Page 50

1. April 5th; Write the date in one week. 2. 7 pints; Multiply the number of cups by the number of days and convert to pints. Use the first part of the analogy to find the number of days (42 cups ÷ 6 cups/day = 7 days). 3. about $\frac{3}{4}$; Write the fraction that represents the number of months out of the year. 4. <; Compare the value of the metric prefixes (centi- = 0.01, kilo- = 1,000). 5. 2,200 grams; Write the number of grams that the cat weighs. Determine from the first part of the analogy that each box weighs 200 grams. Then, multiply 200 grams by 11 boxes.

Page 51

1. $1\frac{1}{3}$; Write the amount of time as a fraction. 2. dollar; A centimeter is $\frac{1}{100}$ of a meter. A penny is $\frac{1}{100}$ of a dollar. 3. volume; Name the measurement that results from multiplying the dimensions of a figure. 4. ; Draw a balance to compare the weight of the heart and the circle based on how each compares to the star. 5. 22 miles; Write the perimeter based on the area from the example (6 × 5 = 30, so L = 6).

Page 52

1. 6 out of 10; Write the ratio of shaded shapes to the total shapes. 2. B is the largest. Name the slice of the pizza that is the largest. 3. 5 out of 9; Write the ratio of seashells to the total shells. 4. Shaded (or gray) is most likely. Write the color of section that the spinner is most likely to land on. 5. 28 grapes, 34 oranges, and 31 cherries; Write the numbers for the tally marks in the frequency table.

Page 53

1. Skate is the most popular. Write the most popular choice. 2. Birds are the fewest. Write the choice that has the fewest number. 3. $\frac{1}{7}$; Write the ratio of Monday to days of the week (1 out of 7). 4. $\frac{3}{7}$; Write the ratio of circles to the total. 5. black & red, black & green, red & green; Write all of the possible color pair combinations.

Page 54

1. range = 60; Calculate the range of the data in the line plot (70 – 10). 2. Pears are the least popular. Write the choice that was least popular. 3. 17 – 1 = 16; Write the equation to calculate the range of the data. 4. impossible; Write the chance for the outcome described. 5. February; Write the month with the most snowy days.

Page 55

1. $\frac{4}{9}$; Write the ratio of Rs to total letters in the group (R because it is the letter that the ratio in the example describes). 2. likely; Describe the likelihood of an outcome for the chance or ratio given. 3. 6 pair combinations; Write the number of pair combinations that can be made with items given. 4. possible or unlikely; Describe the likelihood of the outcome for the amounts given. 5. likely; Describe the likelihood of the outcome.

Page 56

1. $\frac{1}{6}$; Write the ratio or chance of rolling a particular number on a six-sided die. 2. $\frac{7}{15}$; Write the ratio of soccer balls to the total group (soccer balls because it is the option that the ratio in the example describes). 3. 4; Write the mode, or most frequent number, in the data. 4. least likely; Describe the likelihood of choosing red based on the fractions given. 5. 77; Write the mode, or most frequent number, in the data.

Page 57

1. AB, AC, AD, BC, BD, CD; Write all of the pair combinations for the letters given. 2. 8,018; Order the numbers from least to greatest and then write the median, or middle number, in the data. 3. green; Write the mode, or most frequent item, in the data. 4. least; Describe the gray bar in a bar graph that would show the least popular item. 5. ⬤⬤𝇇 ; Draw the number of tennis balls that would be in a pictograph for the data based on the number of games the tennis team won.

Page 58

1. 40; Write the range of the data. 2. OS & GP, OS & BP, BS & GP, BS & BP; Write all of the possible shirt and pants combinations. 3. 10 games; Draw a picture to connect each chess player to every other player just once. 4. 636; Order the numbers from least to greatest and then write the median, or middle number, in the data. 5. decreasing; Describe the change that the line graph shows.

Page 59

1. 19; Write the range of the data. 2. d; Write the mode, or most frequent item, in the data. 3. 28 handshakes; Draw a picture to connect each person to every other person just once. 4. 60; Write the median of the data shown on the line plot. 5.  ; Fill in the Venn diagram with the factors for each number, placing common factors in the overlapping areas.

Page 60

1. 19; Write the mean of the data. 2.  ; Fill in the Venn diagram with the factors for each number, placing common factors in the overlapping areas. 3. YPV, YPW, YGV, YGW, BPV, BPW, BGV, BGW; Write all of the possible clothing combinations.

4.  ; Draw a circle graph for the data in the table. 5. 83; Write the median of the data.